Caribbean Kids Adventure Series

The Twins and the Arawaks

Written and illustrated by

Diafra Thomas-Nunez

Revised

The Twins and the Arawaks

Written and illustrated by

Diafra Thomas-Nunez

Revised

Caribbean Kids Adventures Series
The books in this series are written to introduce children to Caribbean History.
They will read about children who are taken into the past to meet indigenous groups and peoples of the Caribbean and Central America.

Books in the Series

Bella and the Maya
Jamaal Meets Marcus Garvey
Kearra and Mickel meet T. A. Marryshow
The Twins and the Arawaks
Wasani and the Garinagu

About the Author

Diafra Thomas Nunez was born in Grenada, West Indies and as a child, lived in St. Lucia, Trinidad and Grenada. Presently, she lives with her husband and children in Belize, Central America.

She enjoyed reading and from the age of twelve started writing stories of her own. She enjoys working with children and has done so as a teacher and fostering and family placement officer. Her intention for writing this series of books is to contribute to children's literature and so has embarked upon teaching children about the history of the peoples of the Caribbean and Central America in story form.

Table of Contents

Chapter One.....Grandpa's Gift .....Page 7

Chapter Two.......The Arawaks .....Page 13

Chapter Three.....The Cacique......Page 24

Chapter Four..........Farming..........Page 29

Chapter Five.............Batos..........Page 36

Chapter Six........Home Again.......Page 39

Chapter One
Grandpa's Gift

"Grena! Grendon! Come see this!" called Grandpa.

It was a Saturday morning, and two excited children came running outside of their house which was built near the beach.

The twins joined their grandfather who was standing next to an almond tree and staring at a gift he had made for them.

"What is this?" asked Grendon, the eleven year old boy.

"This is a birthday gift. I made this canoe for you both," replied Grandpa, looking down at his grandson.

"Oh Grandpa, it is beautiful!" exclaimed Grena. Her eyes sparkled like the sea water ahead of her.

"Wow, can we take it for a ride?" asked Grendon. He was so happy for their birthday surprise that he could not wait to sail on the ocean.

"I will, but first go tell your mother that we are going to take the canoe out to sea," he told his grandson.

"Yes Grandpa, I will right now," replied Grendon and ran to their house, where Mummy was preparing their breakfast.

"Mummy! Mummy! Guess what, Grandpa made us a canoe for our birthday," said Grendon.

"Oh yes, I know he did, and I guess you want him to take you for a ride in it," said Mammy smiling.

She already knew that the twins would want to try their new canoe.

Mummy had gotten up earlier that day to prepare for their adventure.

She had already made a breakfast picnic basket and was just waiting for the children to come for it.

"Yes Mammy, can we?" asked Grendon.

"Of course you can, that's why I made some sandwiches and lime juice for you already," she said. "Take the basket on the table, there are also some other snacks for you."

"Thanks Mama," said Grendon and gave his mother a tight hug. She looked down at him with her brown eyes and felt very proud. She kissed him on the forehead.

"Now run along, Grena and Grandpa are waiting."

She had so much to do, and was happy that the children would be out for a while. She and their Dad were preparing a surprise birthday party and so it was just a wonderful idea Grandpa had, to take them for a ride in the canoe.

Grendon took the basket of goodies and quickly went back to meet his grandfather and sister on the beach.

The children were ready for their new adventure. They helped their grandfather push the canoe on the sea and then they all climbed in. Grandpa began to paddle.

Oh, what a beautiful sunny day it was. The bright sun made the sea waters sparkle. They sailed past their house and ventured further across the deep blue sea. As they sailed away, the land seemed to get smaller and smaller.

"It is such a lovely day, Grandpa," said Grena dreamily. "Hardly any clouds in the sky and the sea is so calm too, a perfect day for our birthday."

"Yes, and a wonderful day for a ride at sea," agreed Grandpa.

"This is a nice canoe, but where did canoes come from, Grandpa?" asked Grena curiously. She always asked questions as she wanted to know so many things.

"I thought you would never ask. Canoes came from the Amerindians," he answered.

"Who are the Amerindians?" asked Grendon.

"I will not tell you, let me show you one group of these indigenous people," replied Grandpa.
He closed his eyes and said, "Canoe, canoe take us to long ago

lands, to meet some of the Amerindians."

Chapter Two
The Arawaks

Suddenly, the sky became grey and cloudy and a big wave came and took the canoe and its three occupants high into the air and back on the sea. Everything became calm again and the sky became clear and blue.

"What happened?" asked Grendon in a shock. It happened so quickly, that he felt as if he was in a daze.

"You will soon see," answered Grandpa. He continued paddling and soon came to the shore again.

As they neared, everything was different. The children did not see their house anymore; neither did they see any of the other houses or anything from their neighborhood. Something strange was happening.

"Where are we, Grandpa?" asked Grena. She was a little afraid.

"Do not worry, this is a magical canoe. It has taken us back in time to meet an Amerindian group called the Arawaks, who once lived on our islands," said Grandpa.

He did not seem the least bit concerned. As a matter of fact, he was quite happen to arrive at their destination so easily.

They pulled the canoe to a safe spot and started walking.

"Here we will meet and learn about the Arawaks," said Grandpa. "Do not be afraid, they are very friendly people."

"OK Grandpa," said Grena feeling a lot better. She always felt safe with her grandfather and parents.

"Where did the Amerindians come from?" asked Grendon.

"The Amerindians came from South America and settled in the different islands. One of the earlier groups was the Arawaks," Grandpa told the twins. "They would migrate and settle on an island and after a few years they would move again."

"That must have been fun," said Grena. "I wish we can travel like that."

"Let me take you to meet the Cacique," Grandpa told the children.

"Who is the Cacique?" asked Grendon.

"Oh, the Cacique is the chief or leader of the Arawak people," replied Grandpa. He walked ahead and the children followed.

They walked through the trees and bushes up a hill until they came to a little village. It was a long walk, but the children were anxious to meet the Arawak people.

The village was not like the one they grew up in. It was made up of many little hut like houses.

There was only one large rectangular house. The other houses were circular and made of wooden posts put into the ground.

They had cane woven between them and were tied. The houses had no windows or doors, only an opening and their roofs were thatched.

"Wow, look at those houses, "said Grendon. "We are really back in time."

"Yes, the rectangular one belongs to the Cacique. It is called a **Bohio**," said Grandpa to the twins. "It is also the largest house in the village."

"Oh, so the cacique's house has his own special house called a Bohio," said Grena. "Like a king has his castle."

"That is right," confirmed Grandpa.

"What are the round ones called?" asked Grendon.

"Those are called, **caneyes**," answered Grandpa.

"That is interesting, the round houses are called caneyes and the Cacique's house is a bohio," said Grendon. "I never would have thought that their houses had special names."

Something else caught Grena's attention.

"Look Grandpa, there are the Arawak people!" said Grena excitedly.

Ahead of them they saw some of the Amerindian people, the Arawaks.

They were short to medium height and had smooth, olive brown skin. The young ones had black, long hair, while the older ones had grey hair.

"Some have their faces painted and some have their bodies painted too," said Grendon. "They remind me of the Native Americans too, I like to see them."

"Yes, the painting of faces and bodies are part of their culture," said Grandpa.

"See, some of the men have gold ornaments pierced in their noses too," added Grena.

"Yes, they do. Let's go find the cacique," said Grendon. He was fascinated with what he saw and anxious to meet the leader of the Arawaks.

Chapter Three
The Cacique

"Yes, let us go meet the Cacique."

As they walked through, the Arawak people smiled at Grandpa. It was as if they knew him. They were not angry or afraid.

"Hello, Cacique, how are you?" greeted Grandpa when they came to the rectangular house or bohio.

The Arawak leader stood from his chair to welcome his guests.

Welcome back, Grandpa, come in," greeted back the Cacique.

"These are my grandchildren Grena and Grendon," said Grandpa proudly.

"Very nice to meet you Grena and Grendon," said the Cacique.

"Very nice to meet you too," replied the twins in unison.

"My grandchildren want to learn about the Arawak people," said Grandpa.

"Certainly, I will be happy to answer your questions," said the proud leader.

"Do you like being the leader of the people?" asked Grena.

"Oh yes I do!" he answered.

"How did you become the leader?" asked Grendon.

"Oh my father was the leader before me, and his father before him," replied the Cacique.

"Oh, a cacique is the son of a cacique," said Grendon.

"Yes, it is handed down to the eldest son," agreed the Cacique. "Let me get my daughter who can take you around the village."

He called his daughter, Tana. Tana was a little girl of about eleven years.

She was shorter than the twins with long black hair like her father. She also had big, brown eyes.

"Remember Grandpa from a land far away and these are his grandchildren," he said.

The twins said hello to Tana.

"Hello Grandpa, nice to see you again and welcome," greeted Tana.

"Hello Tana, it is great seeing you again," answered Grandpa.

"Please take the children to see

what we do in the village," instructed her father.

"OK Pappy," replied Tana. "What are your names?"

"My name is Grena and this is my brother Grendon," answered Grena.

They became friends quickly and the twins told Tana about their own village.

She was pleased to learn about their home.

Chapter Four
Farming

As they walked out more into the village and down the hill, the twins saw many women planting. They carried a bag of soaked grain around their necks.

"My people do a lot of farming. The women are responsible for planting and preparing food," explained Tana.

"What do they plant?" asked Grendon.

"They plant corn on the hillsides, cassava and yam," answered Tana.

"Is that all you eat?" asked Grendon.

"No, we eat fruits and vegetables too," answered Tana. "We also eat

fish and hunt. We eat manatee, rabbits and birds."

"Can we help plant some too?" asked Grena.

"Of course you can, let us go to the women," said Tana.

The twins walked behind her as she spoke to the women.
They smiled to know that the visitors wanted to help.

The women used sticks to make holes in the ground, threw in the seeds and covered the holes with their feet.

The women gave them a stick each so that they too could make holes in the ground.

Some gave them seeds and they put the seeds into the ground just as the women did and covered the holes with their feet.

Soon they had planted all their seeds.

"That was fun," said Grendon.

They thanked the women for allowing them to help and left with Tana.

The children walked on until they came to a big tree with mangoes on it.

"Can we get some?" asked Grena who was feeling a little hungry.

"Of course, my father is the Cacique and he can get anything he likes and so can I," said Tana smiling.

"Grendon climbed the tree and got three big, ripe juicy mangoes. He gave one each to the others.

After they had eaten, Grendon noticed a house away from the others.

"What is that?" he asked.

"Oh that is the house for our gods or zemis," said Tana.

"How many gods do you have?" asked Grena.

"We have many gods that our priests pray to.

Some of our gods are our ancestors and some are nature. My father is the chief priest and announces the day of the ceremony.

On that day everyone gets prepared by washing and painting our bodies'" said Tana. "We wear our best on that day."

"Oh, I guess it is a special day for your people," said Grendon.

"Yes it is, the priests pray for good fortune for the people, to cure sicknesses, to protect us from our enemies and to help our crops to grow," said Tana.

"So only the priests take part?" asked Grena.

"No, the whole village gathers together and my father leads us to the zemis house. Only my father and the priests go into the hut to pray because not all people can speak to the gods," said Tana.

Tana took them to the area where the people would gather for the ceremony, but they did not go inside the hut.

They stayed for a short while and headed back to the housing area of the village.

Chapter Five
Batos

"What do you do for fun?" asked Grendon.

"Oh, we have a game called batos. My father organizes this game. It is played on a court near my father's house. The ball is specially made of the roots of herbs," said Tana.

"How is it played?" asked Grendon.

"Each side can have as many as twenty players," explained Tana.
"The ball has to be knocked over a line to the opponent's side with any part of the body except the hands."

"The ball must not touch the ground either or go out of the court or else the side will lose points," she told them. They listened keenly.

"That sounds a little like a game we play called volleyball, except we only use our hands." said Grendon.

"Can we go back to Grandpa now so that we can see the court?" asked Grena who was beginning to get tired.

"Of course," said Tana. They followed her back to the Cacique's house. She showed them the court.

They took a ball and tried playing. Tana was very skilled and hardly ever dropped the ball. She used her feet very well.

"It is like playing soccer too," said Grendon. He enjoyed playing Batos.

The Cacique and Grandpa came and joined them. They played with the children for a while too.

"That was fun," said Tana. "You learned very fast."

"Yes it was fun, I will have to teach my friends this game," said Grendon.

They soon were tired of playing and decided to go back to the bohio.

The Cacique ordered a delicious snack of fruit and Grandpa shared the sandwiches they had brought.

Chapter Six
Home Again

After they had finished eating, Cacique and Grandpa chatted for a while.

The children took a walk and Grena picked a flower. She put it on Tana's hair.

Tana smiled.

"I hope you can come visit often," she told the twins.

"Yes, we too," they replied.

"Grena and Grendon, it is getting late and we have to go back home," called Grandpa.

The children went to join the adults.

"Thank you Cacique for an exciting day," said Grandpa to the Cacique.

"It was my pleasure, Grandpa, come back again soon," said the Cacique. He always enjoyed Grandpa's visits.

"Bye Tana, bye Cacique," said the twins.

"Bye," they replied.

The twins had learned so much about the Arawaks and enjoyed their day.

They walked back down the hill and back to the beach to where the canoe was.

Grandpa and the children pulled the canoe to the water.

They jumped inside and Grandpa closed his eyes again and said, "Canoe, Canoe we have to end our roam, please again take us home," he commanded.

The sky again became grey and cloudy and a wave took them high into the air and safely back on the sea. All was calm and in the distance they saw their little house on the beach again.

As Grandpa rowed the canoe to the shore, the children could not wait to go tell their mother what had happened.

They jumped out of the canoe, helped Grandpa put it away. After, they ran to house to tell Mummy all about their adventure.

She smiled as she listened to them tell her about Tana their new friend and her people, the Arawaks.

"Oh Grandpa, they met Tana too, is she still the same size?" asked Mummy.

She too had once visited the Arawak people with her father when she was a little girl.

Grandpa winked at her and smiled.

The End

Made in the USA
Monee, IL
20 September 2021